This Storybook Belongs to:

Princess _Sophie_

Snow White
and the Seven Dwarfs

Enchanted Moments

ADVANCE PUBLISHERS

Once upon a time in a faraway kingdom, there lived a beautiful young woman with hair black as ebony, lips red as a rose, and skin white as snow. Her name was Snow White.

Every day, Snow White drew water from the castle's well. Even though she was a princess, her wicked stepmother, the Queen, treated her like a servant. Snow White was made to scrub the floors and clean the castle.

While she worked, Snow White dreamed of a handsome prince who would someday come and carry her away.

One day, a prince, hearing Snow White's sweet song as he rode by, appeared inside the castle walls. He thought the princess was delightful, but Snow White was too shy to speak to him.

Meanwhile, inside the castle, the wicked Queen stood before her Magic Mirror. She asked the Spirit of the Magic Mirror the same question she repeated every day, "Magic Mirror on the wall, who is the fairest one of all?"

Instead of the answer she expected to hear, the Mirror named someone else—Snow White!

The Queen flew into a jealous rage and summoned her Huntsman to the royal throne room. There she told him to take the princess into the forest and kill her. Then she handed him a carved box. "Bring me back her heart in this!"

The Huntsman took the princess into the forest. But he did not have the heart to harm her. Instead, he told Snow White of the Queen's evil plan. "Run away!" cried the Huntsman. "Run away, hide. Never come back!"

Snow White ran deep into the forest, afraid for her life. The woods seemed strangely alive to her, and everywhere she turned there was something terrifying. Finally, she collapsed, sobbing uncontrollably until she realized that she was frightening the woodland animals. "I'm sorry," she said. "I'm so ashamed."

She asked the animals if they knew where she could go. "I do need a place to sleep at night. Maybe you know where I can stay."

The animals led the princess to a clearing in the woods. There stood a lovely little cottage. Snow White walked up and knocked on the door.

"Hello," called Snow White. "May I come in?"

There was no answer. Slowly, Snow White opened the door and stepped inside. She could hardly believe her eyes. The cottage was a mess.

Luckily, she had her animal friends to help her. In no time, the little cottage was spotless.

Meanwhile, the Seven Dwarfs were on their way home from the diamond mine. Little did they know that the princess was fast asleep upstairs.

They soon discovered her in their beds. The Dwarfs introduced themselves as Sleepy, Grumpy, Happy, Doc, Dopey, Sneezy, and Bashful. When they learned that Snow White could cook, they invited her to stay.

Snow White and the Seven Dwarfs got along very well. They spent their
evenings eating, dancing, and singing.

Even Grumpy took a liking to the kindhearted princess.

Snow White felt at home and happy with her dear new friends.

Back at the castle, the wicked Queen learned that Snow White was still alive. Deep in her dark dungeon, she drank a magic potion that would change her into an old peddler woman.

Then she took an apple and dipped it into another potion. "One taste of the poisoned apple," she said "and Snow White's eyes will close forever!"

Snow White was happily baking pies in the cottage when the old peddler woman appeared at her window.

"Making pies?" asked the old woman, holding out a shiny red apple. "It's apple pies that make the menfolk's mouths water. Pies made from apples like these. Go on. Have a bite."

The birds and animals tried to come to Snow White's rescue. They flew around the old woman's head, fluttering and fussing.

But Snow White shooed her friends away. "Go away, shame on you!" Then she invited the old woman inside.

Frantic, the birds and animals raced off to find the Dwarfs. They knew Snow White was in terrible danger.

The Dwarfs hurried back to the cottage as quickly as they could. But it was too late. They found Snow White lying lifeless on the floor.

Furious, the Dwarfs chased the evil Queen through a pounding rainstorm up a steep and rocky cliff.

When the Queen came to the edge of the cliff, she tried to loosen a boulder that would run the Dwarfs down. Instead, a bolt of lightning struck, causing the Queen to lose her balance and fall to her doom!

Sadly, the Dwarfs built a special bed for Snow White so they could watch over her night and day. They could not bear to part with their loving friend.

Then, one day, a prince from another kingdom appeared. He had heard the story of the beautiful Snow White and hoped that she would be the shy, gentle princess he had met long ago.

When the Prince saw Snow White, his heart filled with love. He knelt down beside her and kissed her.

Snow White opened her eyes and smiled. The Dwarfs cheered happily.

Soon, it was time to go. Snow White kissed each and every Dwarf. She sat atop the Prince's horse and waved good-bye.

Then, the Prince and Snow White rode off to his kingdom where they lived happily ever after.